This book
is prese...
Bo...

WITHDRAWN

-y *Bridget De Franco*
Kindergarten
date 10/21/2002

the Perfect Pet

written by
Carol Chataway

illustrated by
Greg Holfeld

Kids Can Press

For Richard for all his support and his continual badgering
of me to write, and for my three wonderful boys, who have always
wanted a dog but who have somehow ended up with rabbits — C.C.

For Louise, Franklin, Mom, Dad and "poor Bonsai" — G.H.

Published in Canada by
Kids Can Press Ltd.
29 Birch Avenue
Toronto, ON M4V 1E2

Published in the U.S. by
Kids Can Press Ltd.
2250 Military Road
Tonawanda, NY 14150

www.kidscanpress.com

The artwork in this book was rendered in acrylic
and watercolor paints, pencil crayon and ink.
The text is set in New Century Schoolbook.

Printed and bound in Singapore

This book is smyth sewn casebound.

CM 02 0 9 8 7 6 5 4 3 2 1

National Library of Canada Cataloguing in Publication Data

Chataway, Carol, 1955–
The perfect pet

ISBN 1-55337-178-X

1. Pets—Juvenile fiction. I. Holfeld, Greg II. Title.

PZ7.C352Pe 2001   j823   C2001-900600-3

Kids Can Press is a Nelvana company

Hamlet, Pygmalion and Podge wanted a dog more than anything else in the world.

More than ice cream, more than chocolate. Even more than wallowing in mud on a hot summer's day.

Hamlet wanted a calm, patient dog who would wait for him at the gate after school.

Pygmalion wanted a bright, bouncy dog to play with and take on adventures.

And Podge? Podge longed for a warm, cuddly dog to snuggle up with at night.

Every day after school the three little piglets would stop at Mr. Pinkerton's pet shop, peer through the window and sigh.

"You'll frighten my fish with those sad faces," said Mr. Pinkerton kindly. "Can I help you?"

"Oh, Mr. Pinkerton, we want a dog of our own so much," said Hamlet. "But we can't decide what sort to get."

"Hmmm," said Mr. Pinkerton with a low rumbling sound that meant he was thinking hard about the problem. "Why don't you take a dog home today? If it's not what you want, bring it back and we'll try another."

So the three little piglets set off with Goliath.

He was big and noble and bold. But the next day ... When Hamlet came home from school ...

And Pygmalion tried to play ...

And Podge went to bed, well ...

It was AWFUL!

So back they went to the pet shop.

Baxter was bubbly and perky and bright. But the next day …

When Hamlet came home from school …

And Pygmalion set off on an adventure ...

And Podge went to bed, well ...

It was DREADFUL!

So back they went to the pet shop.

Digby looked just right. Soft and gentle and lovable. But …

When Hamlet came home from school …

And Pygmalion went exploring …

And Podge went to bed, well …

It was TERRIBLE!

So back they went to the pet shop.

They tried …

Matilda …

Woodrow …

Buster …

Rover ...

Dotty ...

and Howler ...

It was DISASTROUS!

"Oh, dear!" sighed Hamlet.

"What now?" wailed Pygmalion.

"We'll *never* find a dog of our own," cried Podge. And a large tear rolled off the end of her nose.

"Of course, we will," said Hamlet gently.

"Let's think about this together."

So that night they thought and thought. The next morning they made a list of all the things they liked about dogs and all the things they didn't like.

"Now," said Hamlet, "let's see if Mr. Pinkerton can find us our very own perfect pet."

And back they went to the pet shop.

"Hmmm …" said Mr. Pinkerton with a low rumbling sound that meant he was thinking hard about the problem. "Must be small, clever, playful, friendly, warm, gentle and loving. Must not bark, dig, chew, lick, howl, wander or dribble. Now that's a very unusual dog indeed!"

Hamlet and Pygmalion looked solemnly down at the floor. Podge looked worried.

"Hmmm," he said again. "Come back later.
I'll have to give this some serious thought."

That afternoon the three little piglets hurried back to the pet shop.

"I've found her," said Mr. Pinkerton. "Socks. Your very own perfect pet!"

"She's everything you asked for. Small, clever, playful, friendly, warm, gentle, loving AND guaranteed not to bark, dig, howl or chew!"

And he was right!

The next day when Hamlet came home from school …

And Pygmalion went exploring ...

And Podge went to bed ...

Well ... Socks was just PURRFECT!

Chataway, Carol.
The perfect pet.

$14.95   08/26/2002

DATE			